STAR WARS®

EPISODE I

THE PHANTOM MENACE™

A storybook adapted from the screenplay and story by

GEORGE LUCAS

Interior design by Min Choi

Random House  New York 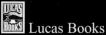 Lucas Books

Very special thanks to

JANE MASON

Senior Editor
Lucas Licensing Ltd.

Additional Acknowledgments

*Sincerest thanks to the wonderful staff at Lucas Licensing Ltd.
and Random House Children's Publishing for their work on this book.*

AT LUCAS LICENSING LTD.:

Lucy Autrey Wilson, *Director of Publishing*
Iain Morris, *Art Editor*
Cara Evangelista and Sarah Hines Stephens

AT RANDOM HOUSE CHILDREN'S PUBLISHING:

Alice Alfonsi, *Editorial Director*
Georgia Morrissey, *Art Director*
Susan Lovelace, *Assistant Art Director*
Kerry Milliron, Artie Bennett,
Christopher Shea, Irene Park,
Fred Pagan, and Carol Naughton.

The Galactic Republic was in turmoil. The greedy Trade Federation wanted control of all trade routes and had unlawfully surrounded the peaceful planet of Naboo with hundreds of giant warships.

Two Jedi Knights—Qui-Gon Jinn and his young apprentice, Obi-Wan Kenobi— were sent by the Republic's Supreme Chancellor, Valorum, to settle the dispute.

As the guardians of peace and justice in the galaxy, Jedi were the perfect choice to handle the difficult situation—before it led to war....

3

"**I** have a bad feeling about this," Obi-Wan Kenobi said to his Master, Qui-Gon Jinn.

The two Jedi Knights waited inside the massive battleship that served as the headquarters for the Trade Federation fleet. Their own vessel was docked in the battleship's vast hangar, and they had been escorted to this conference room by a shiny Federation protocol droid.

Obi-Wan had sensed trouble from the moment they arrived.

"Don't center on your anxiety," Qui-Gon instructed his apprentice. "Be mindful of the living Force. These Trade Federation types are cowards. The negotiations will be short."

In another part of the battleship, the protocol droid was reporting to its masters.

"The ambassadors are Jedi Knights, I believe," the droid announced to the Trade Federation viceroy, Nute Gunray, and his lieutenant Rune Haako, the two Neimoidians in command of the Naboo blockade.

The viceroy glanced at his lieutenant in fear and alarm. Jedi Knights were powerful and wise, and could easily ruin their carefully planned blockade.

Unsure of their next move, the two Neimoidians decided to contact their master, a Sith Lord named Darth Sidious. Within moments, a menacing hologram appeared before them.

"This turn of events is unfortunate," said the flickering image of the evil Sith. "We must accelerate our plans. Begin landing your troops."

"And…the Jedi?" Nute asked.

"The Chancellor should *never* have brought them into this," Darth Sidious said icily. "Kill them immediately."

In the battleship hangar, the Trade Federation cannons aimed at the Jedi's starship.

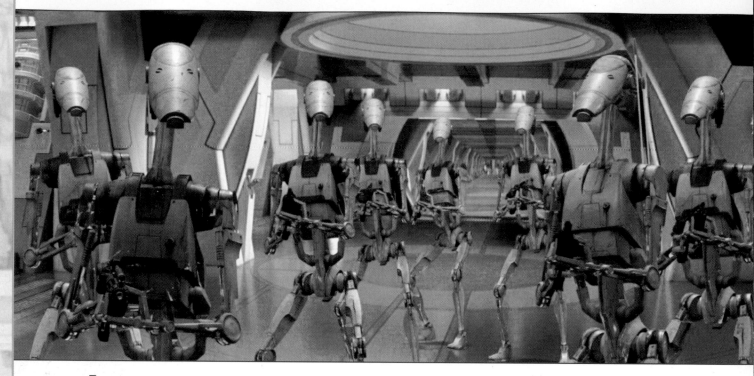

In the conference room, the two Jedi Knights heard a giant explosion, then a low hissing sound.

"Gas!" Qui-Gon cried, jumping to his feet.

Holding their breath, the Jedi drew their lightsabers. A moment later, the conference room door opened, and deadly green fog billowed around them as they stepped into the hallway. Battle droids, firing blasters, blocked their way. The Jedi were under attack!

With lightsabers flashing, the Jedi held their own against the battle droids. But dead ahead, ten large droidekas rolled forward—then transformed into battle position.

"Master!" Obi-Wan warned Qui-Gon. "They have shield generators."

Swiftly, the Jedi escaped the deadly droid attack. But when they finally reached the main hangar, they found that their ship had been destroyed. They were trapped!

From a hidden perch, the Jedi watched the activity in the hangar. Thousands of battle droids were being loaded onto a giant landing craft.

"It's an invasion army," Obi-Wan whispered.

Qui-Gon knew they would have to find a way off this battleship. "We've got to warn the Queen of Naboo that her planet is about to be attacked. And we must contact Chancellor Valorum."

"You were right about one thing, Master," Obi-Wan said. "The negotiations *were* short."

Together, Obi-Wan and Qui-Gon made their escape. They each stole aboard a Trade Federation vessel heading for Naboo. The ships landed in a murky swamp, and the Jedi slipped away.

While Qui-Gon was getting his bearings, a huge troop transport thundered out of the mist—and headed right for him!

Qui-Gon raced through the swamp as frightened animals streaked past him, searching for a place to hide.

Up ahead, a strange-looking creature was squatting in the shallow water, munching on a clam.

"Get out of the way!" Qui-Gon shouted.

The creature looked up, and his eyes went wide. "Oh, nooooooo!" he cried. As Qui-Gon ran by, the terrified creature grabbed on to the Jedi Master. "Hep me! Hep me!" he pleaded.

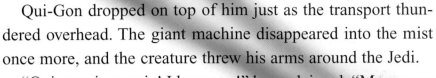

Qui-Gon dropped on top of him just as the transport thundered overhead. The giant machine disappeared into the mist once more, and the creature threw his arms around the Jedi.

"Oyi, mooie-mooie! I luv yous!" he exclaimed. "Mesa yous humble servaunt."

"That won't be necessary," Qui-Gon replied.

But the creature nodded emphatically, his big ears flopping around his head. "Tis demunded byda guds. Tis a live deb-ett, tis. Mesa called Jar Jar Binks."

Qui-Gon wasn't sure exactly what this Jar Jar creature was, but he didn't have much time to wonder. Two flying platforms were suddenly roaring toward them, firing blasters—and chasing Obi-Wan.

"Stay down!" Qui-Gon shouted. Activating his lightsaber, he deflected twin laser bolts—and the platforms exploded in a brilliant blast.

"Yousa sav-ed my again," Jar Jar exclaimed. He looked around warily. "Da motto grande safe place would be Otoh Gunga. Tis safe city."

Qui-Gon and Obi-Wan exchanged looks. "A city," Qui-Gon said. "Can you take us there?"

Jar Jar hesitated. The truth was, he'd been banished from Otoh Gunga. Going back could get him in big trouble. "Terrible tings if my goen back dare," he said.

Just then, a loud rumbling echoed through the swamp. More Trade Federation war machines were coming!

"Dis way!" Jar Jar suddenly cried. "Hurry!"

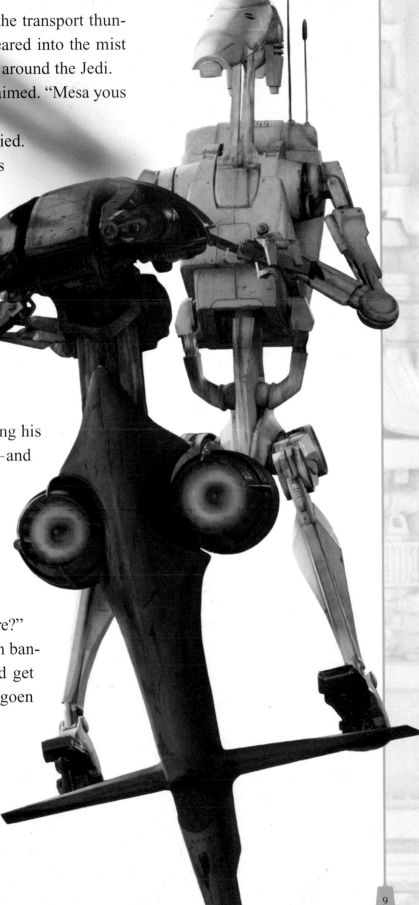

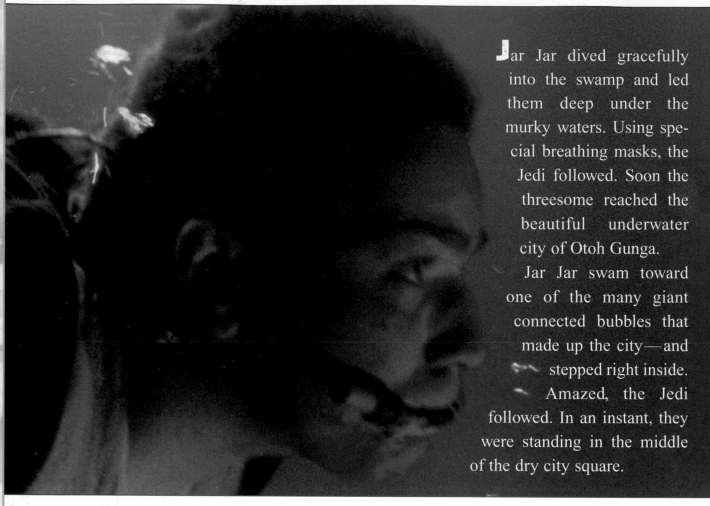

Jar Jar dived gracefully into the swamp and led them deep under the murky waters. Using special breathing masks, the Jedi followed. Soon the threesome reached the beautiful underwater city of Otoh Gunga.

Jar Jar swam toward one of the many giant connected bubbles that made up the city—and stepped right inside.

Amazed, the Jedi followed. In an instant, they were standing in the middle of the dry city square.

Local Gungans scattered at the sight of the Jedi. Guards mounted on huge kaadu quickly surrounded them. The guards pointed their long electropoles at the three dripping visitors.

"Jar Jar, yousa in big dudu dis time," the head guard said, then zapped him with his weapon. Jar Jar leapt into the air.

"How wude!" he complained, rubbing his flanks.

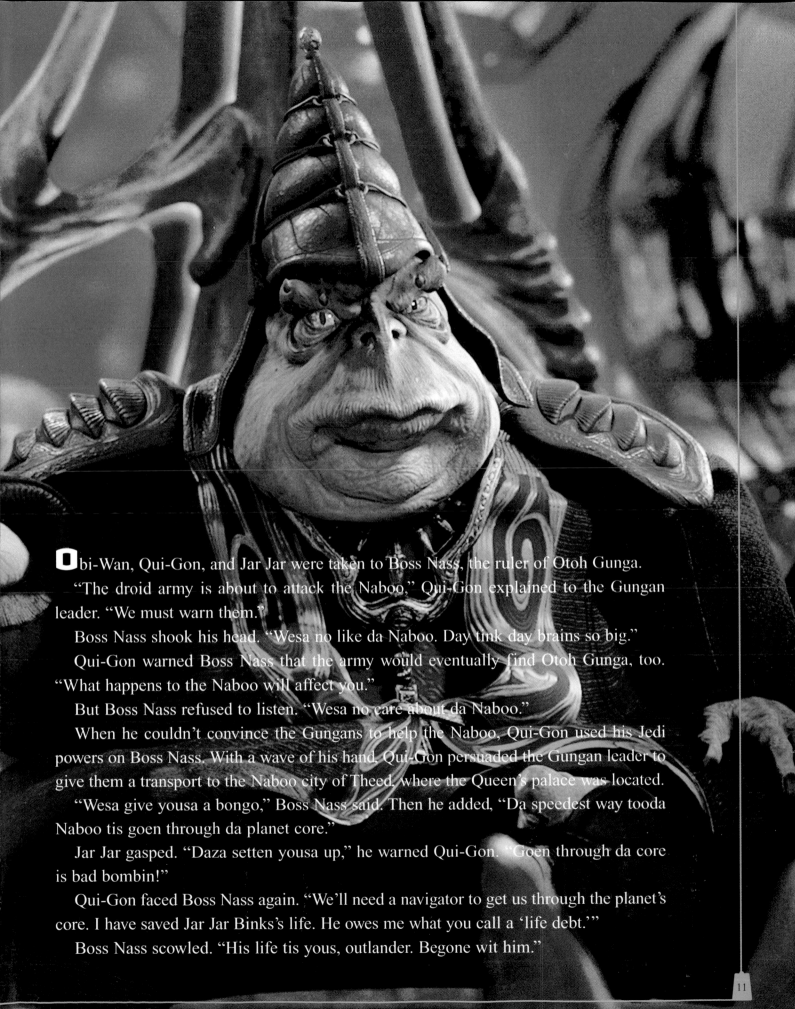

Obi-Wan, Qui-Gon, and Jar Jar were taken to Boss Nass, the ruler of Otoh Gunga.

"The droid army is about to attack the Naboo," Qui-Gon explained to the Gungan leader. "We must warn them."

Boss Nass shook his head. "Wesa no like da Naboo. Day tink day brains so big."

Qui-Gon warned Boss Nass that the army would eventually find Otoh Gunga, too. "What happens to the Naboo will affect you."

But Boss Nass refused to listen. "Wesa no care about da Naboo."

When he couldn't convince the Gungans to help the Naboo, Qui-Gon used his Jedi powers on Boss Nass. With a wave of his hand, Qui-Gon persuaded the Gungan leader to give them a transport to the Naboo city of Theed, where the Queen's palace was located.

"Wesa give yousa a bongo," Boss Nass said. Then he added, "Da speedest way tooda Naboo tis goen through da planet core."

Jar Jar gasped. "Daza setten yousa up," he warned Qui-Gon. "Goen through da core is bad bombin!"

Qui-Gon faced Boss Nass again. "We'll need a navigator to get us through the planet's core. I have saved Jar Jar Binks's life. He owes me what you call a 'life debt.'"

Boss Nass scowled. "His life tis yous, outlander. Begone wit him."

As Qui-Gon and Obi-Wan settled into the small Gungan submarine, Jar Jar looked around worriedly. Jar Jar knew that the dark and murky core was full of giant sea creatures—the kind that would eat anything that came into their path.

"Dis is nutsen," he declared.

"Relax," Qui-Gon replied. "The Force will guide us."

But Jar Jar scoffed, "Oooh, maxibig da Force."

Jar Jar's doubt did not trouble Qui-Gon. Many creatures were skeptical of the Force— until they saw its power for themselves. The Force was an energy field created by all living things. It bound the galaxy together, and the Jedi drew their power from it.

Obi-Wan steered the little submarine through the dark water. The bongo's head-lights lit up no more than a small space in front of them. Beyond that dim light, all was black.

Suddenly, the sub lurched to the side. A huge opee sea killer had hooked the bongo with its gooey tongue!

"Full speed ahead!" Qui-Gon ordered.

A moment later, an even bigger sea creature—a sando aqua monster—emerged from the depths. It chomped the sea killer right in half.

"Wesa free!" Jar Jar proclaimed.

But the little submarine began to lose power. The headlights flickered, and blackness crept in.

"Stay calm," Qui-Gon said as Obi-Wan fiddled with sparking wires. "We're not in trouble yet."

Jar Jar let out a little yelp. "Monstairs out dare, all'n sink'n, and noooo power! When yousa tink wesa in trouble?!"

Just then, the power surged back on, and the headlights lit up.

"Monstair's back!" Jar Jar shouted, pointing ahead.

The lights had startled a giant colo claw fish. It reared back, ready to strike. Obi-Wan turned the bongo around and sped in the other direction...straight toward the jaws of the sando aqua monster!

"This is not good!" Obi-Wan cried. He turned the wheel, and the sub veered to the right, just missing the aqua monster's hungry maw.

Behind them, the colo claw fish was not so lucky. The aqua monster gulped it down.

"There is always a bigger fish," Qui-Gon told his apprentice.

The bongo and its passengers were out of danger. Just as Qui-Gon had predicted, they continued safely through the core and were soon rising toward the surface of Naboo.

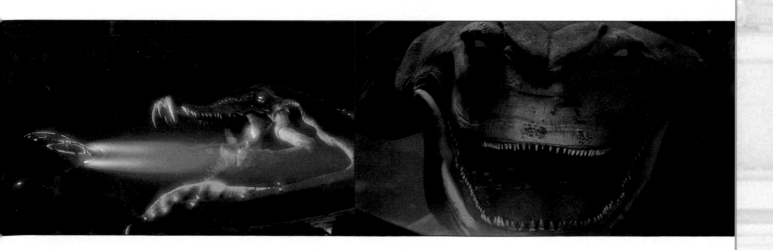

Queen Amidala, the young ruler of Naboo, was in desperate trouble.

Using an army of battle droids, the Trade Federation viceroy had entered her peaceful capital city of Theed and taken over her Royal Palace. Now a slew of battle droids was holding her captive, along with her handmaidens and several of her advisers.

"The Naboo and the Trade Federation will forge a treaty that will make our occupation here legitimate," said the Federation viceroy, Nute Gunray.

"I will not cooperate," the Queen replied defiantly.

"Now, now, Your Highness," the viceroy sneered. "You are not going to like what we have in store for your people." He turned to the droid in charge. "Take them to Camp Four!"

The droid led the captives out of the throne room, toward the detention camp. As they crossed the courtyard, the Queen looked around in horror. Battle droids and tanks were everywhere. Her entire planet was under siege!

Suddenly, Qui-Gon and Obi-Wan leapt from a balcony above.

The battle droids attacked, but the Jedi were too quick for the mechanical soldiers. Drawing their lightsabers, Qui-Gon and Obi-Wan sliced the droids in half.

"We are the ambassadors for the Supreme Chancellor," Qui-Gon quickly explained to the Queen. "We must make contact with the Republic. Do you have transports?"

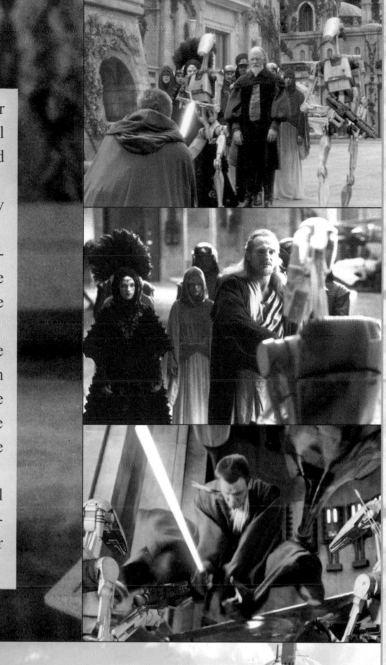

The Queen's group led the Jedi and Jar Jar to Naboo's main hangar, where the Royal Starship awaited them. Qui-Gon implored Queen Amidala to come with them.

"Thank you," said the Queen, "but my place is here with my people."

"The situation is not what it seems," Qui-Gon warned her. "My feelings tell me there is something else behind all this. The Trade Federation will kill you if you stay."

The Queen was soon convinced that the best way to help her people was to go with the Jedi to the planet Coruscant. There she would tell the Galactic Senate about the illegal invasion and find the help her people needed.

Quickly, the Queen boarded her Royal Starship. With her were three of her handmaidens; Captain Panaka, the head of her security forces; the Jedi; and Jar Jar Binks.

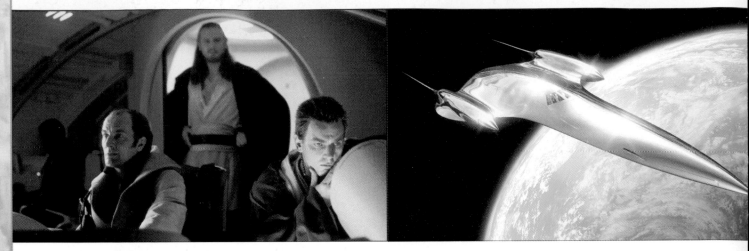

"**H**ang on!" the ship's captain said as the sleek Royal Starship streaked skyward.

The Queen's transport was very fast, but it was not a warship. It had no weapons. They were completely defenseless as they approached the Trade Federation's deadly blockade far above the planet's surface.

Laser fire came at them from all sides. An alarm sounded throughout the ship. They had been hit!

"We've lost our shields!" the captain warned.

Instantly, a team of R2 repair droids were sent out onto the ship's hull. The droids worked quickly, but the Trade Federation attack was unrelenting. One by one, the R2 units were blasted off the hull.

Only a single droid remained. At the very last moment, the little blue droid reconnected the damaged wires, and the starship's shields were restored. The Queen's ship raced past the blockade and into the safety of deep space.

The little blue droid had saved them!

"What is its number?" asked the Queen when the droid rolled back inside. "It is to be commended."

Captain Panaka read the droid's panel. "Artoo-Detoo," he said.

Darth Sidious was furious when he learned that the Queen had escaped Naboo and the Jedi were still alive.

"Find her!" he bellowed to the viceroy. "I want that treaty signed!"

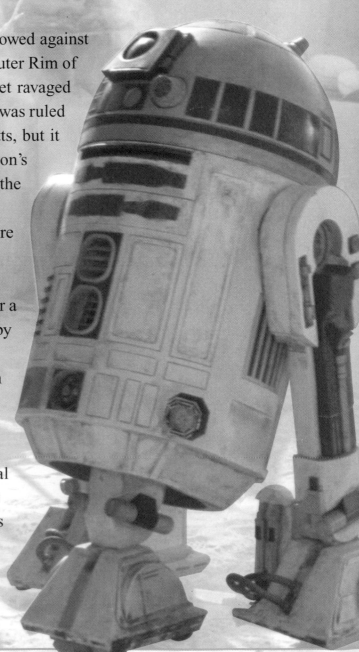

Meanwhile, back on the Royal Starship, the Queen learned that her ship's hyperdrive had been damaged in the attack. Without repairs, the Naboo ship would never make it to Coruscant.

Ahead of them, a dusty brown planet glowed against the dark curtain of space. Located in the Outer Rim of the galaxy, Tatooine was a hot desert planet ravaged by the heat of twin suns. The remote world was ruled by a race of crime lords known as the Hutts, but it was also far away from the Trade Federation's influence—and that was good news to the Jedi and the Queen.

She agreed to have her ship land there immediately for emergency repairs.

After touching down, Qui-Gon arranged for a small landing party to hike into the nearby spaceport of Mos Espa.

While the rest of the group stayed with the ship, Qui-Gon, Jar Jar, and R2-D2 set off. At the Queen's insistence, one of her handmaidens—a pretty girl named Padmé—went along to observe the local culture.

Before long, the foursome came across a cluttered junk shop that sold used ship parts.

"**W**hat do you want?" the unpleasant owner snapped in Huttese as the group entered his dingy shop. The blue Toydarian darted back and forth on two stubby wings. His name was Watto.

Qui-Gon explained that he was looking for parts. Watto shouted something over his shoulder. A moment later, a small, dirty boy appeared, dressed in ragged clothing.

"Watch the store," Watto commanded the boy. "I've got some selling to do." With that, Watto, Qui-Gon, and R2-D2 left the shop and headed for the junkyard out back.

"Are you an angel?" the disheveled boy asked Padmé after the others left the junk shop.
The Queen's handmaiden was surprised. "What?"

"Are you an angel?" the boy repeated, staring at her. "I've heard deep space pilots talk
about them. Angels are the most beautiful creatures in the universe."

Padmé blushed. "You're a funny little boy," she said. "How do you know so much?"

"I listen to all the traders and pilots who come through here," the boy replied.

"Have you been here long?" Padmé asked.

"Since I was very little," the boy answered. "My mom and I were sold to Gardulla the
Hutt, but she lost us to Watto betting on the Podraces."

"You're a slave?" Padmé couldn't hide her surprise. Slavery had been outlawed
throughout most of the galaxy.

The little boy scowled. "I'm a person!" he cried. "My name is Anakin Skywalker."

"I'm sorry," Padmé said quickly. "I don't fully understand. This is a strange world to me."

Outside the junk shop, Qui-Gon was pleased to learn that Watto had the parts he needed. But when Watto heard that Qui-Gon intended to pay for them with Republic credits, he put a stop to the deal.

"Republic credits are no good out here," Watto scoffed.

As he'd done with Boss Nass, the Jedi Master waved his hand before Watto's face. The Force could often be used to influence the weak-minded. "Republic credits will do fine," he said to Watto.

But the Toydarian shook his head stubbornly. "No, they won't."

The Jedi tried his powers again, this time waving his hand a bit higher. "Credits will do fine," Qui-Gon repeated.

"You think you're some kinda Jedi, waving your hand around like that?" Watto scoffed. "I'm a Toydarian. Mind tricks don't work on me—only money! No money, no parts, no deal!"

Young Anakin Skywalker was sorry to see Padmé and her friends leave Watto's junk shop. But as luck would have it, he saw them later that day in the marketplace, just as a dangerous sandstorm was blowing into town. The group needed shelter, and Anakin invited them back to his slave quarters.

"Mom! I'm home!" Anakin shouted as the group came through the door.

Shmi Skywalker was surprised to see her small home invaded by outlanders.

"These are my friends," Anakin said.

"Your son was kind enough to offer us shelter," Qui-Gon told Shmi. "He's a very special boy."

Shmi gave Qui-Gon a meaningful look. "Yes, I know."

Happy to have visitors, Anakin could hardly wait to show off some of his inventions. He took Padmé to his small room and showed her the protocol droid he was building to help his mother around the house. It had no outer coverings, but it was already working very well.

"He's wonderful!" Padmé exclaimed.

Anakin pushed a switch and the droid sat up. "How do you do?" said the droid in a stiff voice. "I am See-Threepio. How may I serve you?"

From across the room, R2-D2 chirped and beeped.

"I beg your pardon," C-3PO replied. "What do you mean, I'm naked? What's naked?"

"Vooo, dwip, whoop," R2-D2 answered.

"Oh, my goodness!" C-3PO exclaimed, aghast. "How embarrassing!"

Anakin grinned. "Don't worry," he assured the mortified droid. "I'll fix that soon enough."

Outside, fierce winds whipped across the desert. Gritty brown drifts piled higher and higher against the buildings of Mos Espa. Soon sand covered everything in sight.

Inside the Skywalker hovel, Anakin and his mother ate a simple dinner with their new friends.

"I can't believe there is still slavery in the galaxy," Padmé said. "The Republic's anti-slavery laws—"

"The Republic doesn't exist out here," Shmi explained sadly. "We must survive on our own."

There was a moment of awkward silence.

"Have you ever seen a Podrace?" Anakin suddenly asked. "I'm the only human who can pilot a Pod."

"You must have Jedi reflexes if you can race Pods," Qui-Gon observed.

Anakin gazed at Qui-Gon intently. "You're a Jedi Knight, aren't you?"

Qui-Gon had been trying to hide his identity on Tatooine, but he knew there was no fooling this young boy.

"We're on our way to Coruscant on an important mission," Qui-Gon confessed, "and it must be kept secret."

Padmé explained that their ship was damaged, and that they had no money to buy replacement parts. "These junk dealers must have a weakness of some kind," she said thoughtfully.

Shmi nodded. "Gambling. Everything on Tatooine revolves around those awful Podraces."

Anakin's face lit up. "I've built a Pod!" he told Qui-Gon. "There's a big race tomorrow. You could enter it! You could make Watto think the Pod was yours and get him to let me pilot it for you."

Shmi looked upset. "I don't want you to race, Annie. It's awful."

"But we have to help them, Mom," Anakin pleaded. "You said that the biggest problem in the universe is that no one helps each other."

"I'm sure Qui-Gon doesn't want to put your son in danger," Padmé told Shmi. "We'll find some other way."

Shmi shook her head. "There is no other way," she admitted. "I may not like it, but he can help you…he was meant to help you."

At the junk shop the next morning, Anakin watched Qui-Gon make his wager with Watto.

Pretending Anakin's Podracer was his own, Qui-Gon told Watto that he wanted to enter the race using Anakin as his driver. "If we win," Qui-Gon told Watto, "you keep all of the winnings, minus the cost of the parts I need. If we lose, you keep my ship."

Watto thought about Qui-Gon's proposal for a moment. He gazed at the hologram of the sleek starship, projected from Qui-Gon's holoprojector.

"Either way, you win," Qui-Gon said.

"It's a deal!" Watto exclaimed, his eyes shining with greed.

Anakin felt a rush of excitement. The bet was on!

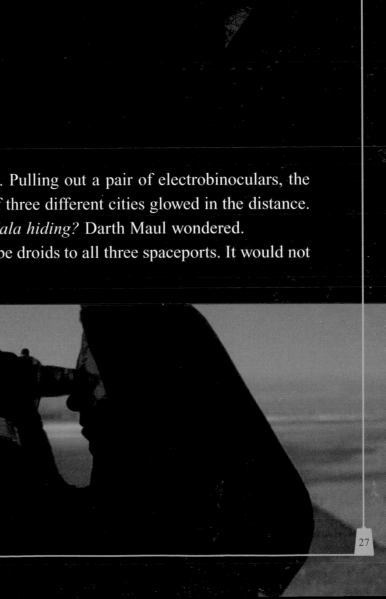

In another part of the galaxy, Darth Sidious had taken matters into his own hands. If the viceroy couldn't find the Queen and her two Jedi protectors, he knew who could—his Sith apprentice, Darth Maul.

"Move against the Jedi first," Sidious instructed Maul. "You will then have no difficulty taking the Queen back to Naboo, where she will sign the treaty."

Darth Maul smiled wickedly. "At last we will reveal ourselves to the Jedi," he hissed. "At last we will have revenge."

Darth Sidious nodded under his dark hood. "You have been well trained, my young apprentice. They will be no match for you."

That night, while everyone slept, a strange spacecraft landed in a remote stretch of the Tatooine desert. As it touched down, a herd of wild banthas scattered in all directions.

A lone figure soon emerged from the ship. Pulling out a pair of electrobinoculars, the dark man scanned the landscape. The lights of three different cities glowed in the distance.

In which city are the Jedi and Queen Amidala hiding? Darth Maul wondered.

The Sith apprentice quickly dispatched probe droids to all three spaceports. It would not take long to find them now!

The day of the big Podrace was here! The twin suns shone high in the sky, heating up the racecourse. The grandstand was packed with spectators from all over the galaxy.

As the racers lined up at the starting grid, a two-headed announcer greeted the fans, welcoming them to the Boonta Eve Race, the most hazardous of all Podraces. "Our glorious host, Jabba the Hutt, has entered the arena. It won't be long now before we begin this grueling contest."

Anakin Skywalker was excited—and a little nervous—as he approached his Podracer. He knew he was a good racer. He knew he could win. But he also knew he'd never won before—in fact, he'd never even *finished* a race.

Something deep inside Anakin told him that winning *this* race was more important than winning all of those other races. More important than *anything* he'd ever done before.

"Be safe," his mother begged as he strapped on his helmet.

"May da guds be kind, mesa palo," Jar Jar added.

"You carry all our hopes," Padmé reminded him.

Then Sebulba, a racer from the planet Malastare, elbowed his way over to Anakin.

"You won't walk away from this one, slave scum," he taunted in his Dug language. "You're bantha poodoo!"

Anakin glared at Sebulba. The Dug was the most successful Podracer on Tatooine. He was also the nastiest. Anakin had raced Sebulba before and knew he was a cheater and a bully. This time, Anakin was determined *not* to let the wily Dug get the best of him.

"Are you all set, Annie?" Qui-Gon asked as he approached the boy's Podracer.

Anakin nodded as he belted himself in.

"Remember," Qui-Gon said, "concentrate on the moment. Feel, don't think. Use your instincts." He smiled as he stepped away. "May the Force be with you."

The racers started their engines, and the roar of the powerful machines filled the arena.

"And they're off!" the announcer cried. Then he blinked in surprise. "Wait, little Skywalker has stalled at the starting line!"

Inside his cockpit, Anakin yanked the thruster bars back to neutral and cleared his fuel lines. Then he flipped a switch and blasted out of the starting grid after the other racers.

Out on the course, the roar of engines was deafening. Sebulba and a racer named Mawhonic were running neck and neck for the lead. All of a sudden, Sebulba rammed his Podracer into Mawhonic's, sending him crashing into a rocky canyon wall.

Fire and smoke filled the air as Mawhonic's racer exploded.

At the back of the pack, Anakin sped past a Podracer—then another and another. But a racer named Gasgano wouldn't let Anakin pass. Anakin tried the right side, then the left. Finally, Gasgano went over a cliff drop-off. Anakin gunned his engines and sailed right over him!

"Wow!" Anakin exclaimed as he zoomed onward, passing racers left and right.

Up ahead, Sebulba was still in the lead. But another racer, Xelbree, was hot on his tail. Sebulba let Xelbree come up alongside him. Then he cut through Xelbree's engine tethers with a powerful blast of exhaust.

Kaboom! Xelbree's Podracer exploded in a shower of sparks.

Sebulba deftly veered away and zoomed toward the arena.

"Here comes Sebulba in record time!" the announcer cried.

The crowd cheered as racers tore through the arena—two more laps to go! But where was Anakin?

In the stands, Shmi worriedly scanned the course for any sign of her son.

"He musta crash-ed," Jar Jar said gloomily.

"Here he comes!" Padmé cheered.

Anakin had steered his Podracer around the bend and was roaring through the arena. He was gaining on the pack!

But up ahead, Sebulba was ready to take on any challenger. As Anakin moved closer, the Dug broke off a small part of his racer and sent it careening into Terter's. Terter swerved straight into Anakin!

Anakin tried not to panic as his Podracer veered about wildly. Sebulba was getting away! The Dug raced through the arena again as Anakin tried to catch up. Only one lap to go!

Anakin hit the thrusters. Soon he and Sebulba were running neck and neck, roaring over the rough desert terrain. Then Sebulba blasted Anakin's Podracer with exhaust, forcing Anakin through a service gate and off the course!

Anakin concentrated hard as his Podracer twisted and turned high in the air. On a tight corner, he dived to the inside and zoomed back onto the course—in front of Sebulba!

"A controlled thrust and he's back on course!" the announcer exclaimed. "What a move!"

Desperate to win, the Dug came up alongside Anakin. He veered his Podracer into Anakin's, and their steering rods hooked together. Anakin tried to pull away, and his steering rod broke altogether. Sebulba's Podracer flew free and Anakin's began to spin!

Gripping his thrusters, Anakin quickly regained control of his Podracer. But where was Sebulba?

Crash! Sebulba's engines hit the ground with a huge explosion. As the Dug's cockpit skidded to an abrupt halt, he let out an angry shriek. He'd lost the Podrace to a human boy!

Anakin streaked ahead, his eyes focused on one thing: the finish line. As he crossed it, the crowd went wild.

Anakin Skywalker had won the Boonta Eve Race!

Anakin beamed as his cheering friends gathered around him. He'd done it! He'd won!

When they returned to the Skywalker slave quarters, Qui-Gon revealed a secret. Anakin had won more than just the ship parts from Watto. He'd also won his freedom.

"You're no longer a slave," Qui-Gon announced. The Jedi had made a secret bet with Watto on the morning of the race—a bet for Anakin's freedom.

Anakin's mother gasped in surprise. "Will you take him with you?" she asked. "Is he to become a Jedi?"

Qui-Gon explained that Anakin was extraordinarily strong in the Force, but he would have to be tested by the Jedi Council. The Masters of the Council would decide the boy's fate.

"Training to be a Jedi will not be easy," Qui-Gon warned Anakin. "And if you succeed, it will be a hard life."

Anakin didn't hesitate. "I want to go," he said. He turned to pack his things, then stopped and faced Qui-Gon.

"What about Mom?" he asked. "Is she free, too?"

Qui-Gon shook his head. "I tried to free your mother, but Watto wouldn't have it."

Shmi smiled bravely. "Son, my place is here. My future is here. It is time for you to let go...and make your dreams come true."

"I want to stay with you," Anakin cried. "I don't want things to change."

"You can't stop change any more than you can stop the suns from setting. Listen to your feelings, Annie. You know what is right."

Anakin tried to be brave, but inside he was sad.

If only Mother could come with us! he thought. *Then everything would be perfect.*

While Padmé, Jar Jar, and R2-D2 went back to the ship with the newly won parts, Anakin packed and said good-bye to C-3PO and his friends. But when it came time to leave his mother, his eyes filled with tears.

"I can't do it, Mom," he sobbed.

Shmi gave her son a reassuring hug. "This is one of those times when you have to do something you don't think you can do," she explained. "I know how strong you are, Annie. I know you can do this."

Anakin swallowed hard. "I...I will come back here and free you, Mom... I promise."

Shmi nodded and gave her son one last hug. "Now be brave, and don't look back."

"I love you so much," Anakin said. Then he wiped the tears out of his eyes and followed Qui-Gon away from his home and his mother.

He did not look back.

Qui-Gon was eager to leave Tatooine.

He led Anakin out of Mos Espa and toward the newly repaired Naboo starship. But trouble was not far behind them. One of the Sith probe droids had tracked the Jedi down.

Before Qui-Gon and Anakin could reach the ship, Darth Maul zoomed up behind them on his speeder bike. Leaping off the vehicle, Maul raised his lightsaber and swung, but Qui-Gon blocked the blow.

"Annie, get to the ship!" Qui-Gon shouted as the two warriors began to fight. "Tell them to take off! Go! Go!"

Anakin raced toward the ship. "Qui-Gon's in trouble!" he told the others on board. "He says to take off...now!"

Obi-Wan Kenobi gazed through the cockpit's viewport. "Over there!" he cried, spotting a cloud of dust in the distance. "Take off and fly low!" he commanded the pilot.

Outside, Qui-Gon and Darth Maul battled on. Energy crackled as their weapons clashed. They leapt over one another and twisted in the air, each trying to gain the advantage.

As the ship approached them, they both looked up. In a flash, Qui-Gon leapt to the spacecraft ramp. Darth Maul tried to follow, but Qui-Gon knocked him back onto the desert floor.

Exhausted, Qui-Gon collapsed inside the closed hatch, visibly shaken.

"Are you all right?" Anakin asked worriedly.

"I think so," Qui-Gon gasped as he tried to catch his breath. "But that was a surprise I won't soon forget."

"What was it?" Obi-Wan asked his Master.

"I don't know...but he was well trained in the Jedi arts," Qui-Gon replied. "I think it was a Sith Lord."

Anakin's eyes grew wide. "What are we going to do?" he asked.

"We will be patient," Qui-Gon replied. Then he turned his gaze to his apprentice. "Anakin Skywalker, meet Obi-Wan Kenobi."

The Royal Starship traveled quickly to the shimmering city-planet of Coruscant. There, the Queen met with Naboo's Senator, Palpatine.

"I must be frank, Your Majesty," he told her. "There is little chance the Senate will act on the invasion. Supreme Chancellor Valorum has no power—the bureaucrats are in charge now."

The Queen sighed. She had come a long way in the hopes that the Senate would help her people. Since she'd left her planet, the Trade Federation had tightened its grip on Naboo. Her people were suffering…dying. Their only hope was for the Senate to act.

"What options do we have?" she asked.

"Our best choice is to force a new election for a stronger Supreme Chancellor," Senator Palpatine said very carefully. "We must remove Valorum and elect a Chancellor who will take control, enforce the laws, and give us justice."

The Queen did not like the idea of turning against Chancellor Valorum. He had always been good to her people—and to her. But her planet was suffering.

Queen Amidala knew what she had to do. Without delay, the Queen and Senator Palpatine took Naboo's case before the Senate. But the Senate was caught up in politics and could not move to resolve the situation.

"I was not elected to watch my people suffer and die while you debate this invasion in a committee," Queen Amidala said angrily. "If this body is not capable of action, I suggest new leadership is needed. I move for a vote of no confidence in Chancellor Valorum."

Chancellor Valorum went pale as the chamber erupted into a roar of approval and jeers. Stunned, Valorum turned toward Senator Palpatine.

"You have betrayed me!" he cried accusingly.

Not far away, in the spire of the Jedi Temple, Qui-Gon Jinn was finishing his report to the Jedi Council. Obi-Wan Kenobi stood by his Master, listening as intently as the Council members.

"…my only conclusion can be that it was a Sith Lord," said Qui-Gon after describing his mysterious attacker.

The Sith followed the dark side of the Force. They were evil and would do almost anything to secure their power.

"Impossible!" Ki-Adi-Mundi, one of the Council members, cried. "The Sith have been extinct for a millennium."

"I do not believe the Sith could have returned without us knowing," said Mace Windu, a senior Jedi on the Council.

"Hard to see, the dark side is," Jedi Master Yoda said quietly. "With this Naboo Queen you must stay, Qui-Gon. Protect her. May the Force be with you."

Obi-Wan turned to leave, but Qui-Gon had something else he needed to speak about—Anakin Skywalker.

"With your permission, my Master," he said to Yoda. "I have encountered a vergence in the Force."

"Located around a person?" Mace Windu asked.

"A boy," Qui-Gon explained. "His cells have the highest concentration of midi-chlorians I have seen in a life form. I request the boy be tested. Finding him was the will of the Force."

"Bring him before us, then," Mace Windu said.

Anakin Skywalker was taken before the Council members. Mace Windu watched a small viewing screen that faced away from Anakin. Images flashed across it in the blink of an eye.

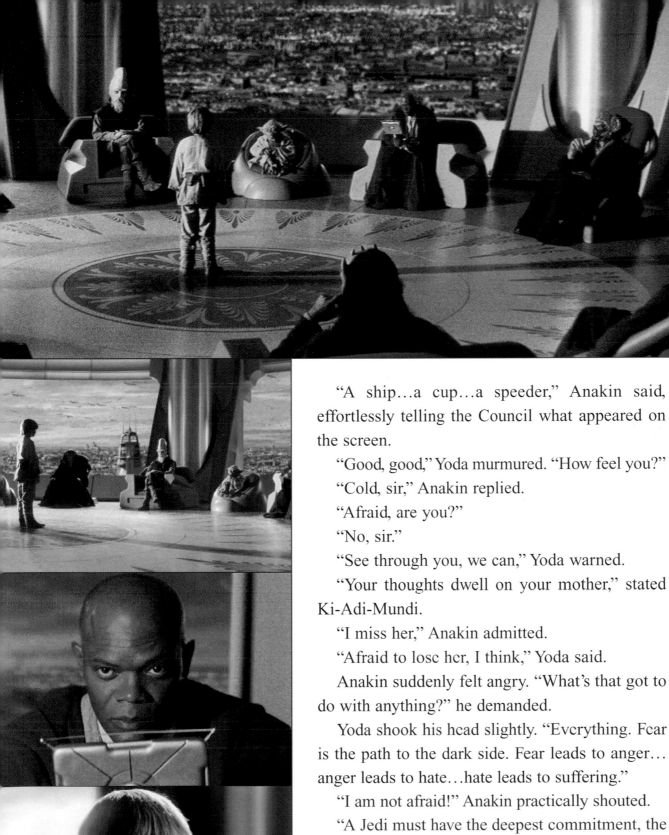

"A ship…a cup…a speeder," Anakin said, effortlessly telling the Council what appeared on the screen.

"Good, good," Yoda murmured. "How feel you?"

"Cold, sir," Anakin replied.

"Afraid, are you?"

"No, sir."

"See through you, we can," Yoda warned.

"Your thoughts dwell on your mother," stated Ki-Adi-Mundi.

"I miss her," Anakin admitted.

"Afraid to lose her, I think," Yoda said.

Anakin suddenly felt angry. "What's that got to do with anything?" he demanded.

Yoda shook his head slightly. "Everything. Fear is the path to the dark side. Fear leads to anger… anger leads to hate…hate leads to suffering."

"I am not afraid!" Anakin practically shouted.

"A Jedi must have the deepest commitment, the most serious mind," Yoda explained. "I sense much fear in you."

Anakin stood firm. "I am not afraid," he said again.

"Then continue, we will," Yoda said.

After Anakin's testing was over, the Jedi Council members called Anakin, Qui-Gon, and Obi-Wan to stand together before them.

"The Force is strong with him," Ki-Adi-Mundi told Qui-Gon.

Qui-Gon smiled. "He is to be trained, then."

"No," Mace Windu stated. "He is too old—there is already much anger in him."

Crestfallen, Anakin felt his eyes fill with tears.

"But he is the chosen one," Qui-Gon protested. "You must see it."

"Clouded, this boy's future is," Yoda said.

"I will train him, then," Qui-Gon said willfully.

The words stunned Obi-Wan. Qui-Gon already had one apprentice—him—and it was forbidden to take on a second Padawan.

"Now is not the time for this," Mace Windu told Qui-Gon. "The Senate is voting for a new Supreme Chancellor. Queen Amidala has decided to return to her planet. Go with her to Naboo and discover the identity of this dark warrior. That is the clue we need to unravel this mystery of the Sith."

Yoda agreed. "Young Skywalker's fate will be decided later."

"I brought Anakin here," Qui-Gon pointed out. "He must stay in my charge."

"Take him with you," Yoda warned, "but train him not!"

On the Royal Starship, the Queen approached Jar Jar Binks. She asked him to help her make peace with the Gungans.

Jar Jar agreed, and after they landed on Naboo, he swam down to the Gungans' underwater city. But all he found was an empty plaza. The Trade Federation had attacked Otoh Gunga, and the Gungans had fled to a secret hiding place—a ruined temple.

Fortunately, Jar Jar knew how to find it.

Unfortunately, the Gungans were not happy to be found.

When Jar Jar, the Queen, and her entourage arrived at the sacred temple ruins, they were quickly surrounded by Gungan guards.

Queen Amidala stepped forward and spoke to Boss Nass in a shaky voice. "I am Queen Amidala of the Naboo. W-we come in peace," she stammered.

"Yousa all bombad," Boss Nass growled at the unsteady Queen. He mistakenly believed that the Naboo were to blame for the Trade Federation invasion. "Yousa all die'n, mesa tink."

Suddenly, one of the Queen's handmaidens stepped forward. "Your Honor," Padmé said loudly, "*I* am Queen Amidala."

Everyone gasped. Padmé was really the Queen!

She pointed to the young woman dressed in the Queen's clothes. "This woman is my decoy. I am sorry for the deception, but under the circumstances it was necessary to protect myself."

The real Queen paused for a moment. "Your Honor, our two great societies have always lived in peace," she said. "The Trade Federation has destroyed all that we have worked so hard to build. I beg you to help us."

Amidala dropped to her knees before Boss Nass, and her handmaidens gasped at the act. "We are your humble servants," she said. "Our fate is in your hands."

Then, one by one, the rest of the Queen's followers dropped to their knees before the Gungan leader.

Boss Nass looked pleased. "Yousa no tinken yousa greater den da Gungans." He paused for a moment. "Mesa like dis. Maybe wesa bein friends," he said, and agreed to use his army to help the Naboo. Then he turned to the outcast Jar Jar Binks.

"And wesa maken yousa Bombad General!" Boss Nass told Jar Jar.

"General!? In da army?!" Jar Jar exclaimed. His tongue flopped out and he fell to the ground in a dead faint.

After Jar Jar was revived, the Queen discussed her battle plans with the Gungan generals, the Jedi, and her Naboo officers.

"We have to draw the battle droids away from the Naboo cities," she explained. "Then we can get to the palace and capture the viceroy. Without the Trade Federation leader, the army will be lost and confused."

"It is possible that many Gungans will be killed," Qui-Gon warned.

"Wesa ready to do are-sa part," Boss Nass said with confidence.

Hearing this, Jar Jar began to feel woozy again. He was no warrior!

"We also have a plan that will stop the droid army in their tracks," the Queen continued. "The droids are all guided by a Control Ship orbiting the planet. If our Naboo starfighters can destroy that ship, we will sever all communication with the droid army. Without guidance, the droids will be helpless."

Amidala looked into the faces of everyone around her. "We must not fail," she said.

Not far away, Darth Sidious's menacing presence chilled the palace throne room. "She is more foolish than I thought," he declared.

The Trade Federation viceroy, his lieutenant, and Darth Maul watched the Dark Lord's hologram pace the floor.

"We are sending all available troops to meet this army of hers," Nute Gunray explained to his master. "We do not expect much resistance."

Darth Sidious looked almost pleased. "Wipe them out," he commanded. "All of them."

Meanwhile, hundreds of Gungan warriors emerged from a Naboo swamp lake.

Most of the soldiers were mounted on two-legged kaadu. But others rode lizardlike fambaas with large shield generators strapped to their backs.

They were ready for battle.

Inside the Theed palace, Qui-Gon, Obi-Wan, and Anakin carefully made their way to the main hangar with the Queen, her handmaidens, and Captain Panaka. But the Trade Federation battle droids were waiting for them.

Suddenly, there was blaster fire everywhere!

"Get to your ships!" the Queen called to the pilots. Several Naboo pilots jumped into their starfighters and blasted their way out of the hangar.

Qui-Gon turned to Anakin. "Find a safe place to hide and stay there."

Anakin jumped into the empty cockpit of a starfighter. R2-D2 chirped behind him. The little blue droid had been loaded into the very starfighter Anakin had chosen to hide in!

Amid the chaos in the hangar, everyone moved toward the exit. Suddenly, a dark shadow fell over the group—it was cast by the mysterious figure who had attacked Qui-Gon on Tatooine!

Captain Panaka, the Queen, and her troops backed away in alarm.

"We'll handle this," Qui-Gon said.

He and Obi-Wan dropped their capes and activated their lightsabers.

Darth Maul drew his own lightsaber, igniting both ends to create a deadly, double-bladed weapon.

Lightsabers flashed as the two Jedi tried to overcome their fierce opponent. But Darth Maul had been well trained, and with his double-bladed lightsaber, he was a powerful enemy.

Sabers hummed and clashed as the three warriors moved out of the hangar and into a power generator pit. Darth Maul leapt up onto a catwalk and the Jedi followed.

With a swift kick, Darth Maul forced Obi-Wan off the catwalk.

Qui-Gon raised his lightsaber and delivered a strong blow. Caught off balance, Darth Maul fell from the catwalk and landed hard. The Jedi quickly leapt at him, but Darth Maul was already on his feet. He jumped through a small door.

Qui-Gon followed, and Obi-Wan raced to catch up. The Jedi found themselves in a narrow hallway full of electron rays. The rays switched on and off every minute or so, creating deadly walls of energy.

Darth Maul ran down the corridor. Qui-Gon had almost caught the Sith Lord when the beams activated. Shimmering walls of pure energy stopped all three warriors in their tracks. Each was locked in an electronic cell.

In front of Qui-Gon, Darth Maul used the break in the battle to catch his breath. Behind him, Obi-Wan paced impatiently. Qui-Gon chose to kneel and meditate. They would all have to wait until the beams switched off again.

Only then would the battle continue.

From inside the cockpit of the Naboo starfighter, Anakin watched six giant droidekas roll into the hangar, transform into deadly battle position, and advance toward the Queen!

"We gotta do something, Artoo," Anakin said to the little blue droid. "Where's the trigger?" he asked, pushing a button. Suddenly, the starfighter lurched to the side. "Oops, wrong one!" he said, and pushed another button. This time, the lasers fired, blasting several droidckas.

As the startled droids turned to look for their attacker, the Queen and her followers escaped into the hallway.

R2-D2 whistled a cheer.

"Yeah, all right, droid blaster. Yeah!" Anakin agreed.

But a moment later, the droids began firing on Anakin's starfighter! He flipped some more switches. The engines roared and the ship began to shake.

"Oops! Wrong one!"

A moment later, Anakin's starfighter rocketed out of the hangar and headed into space!

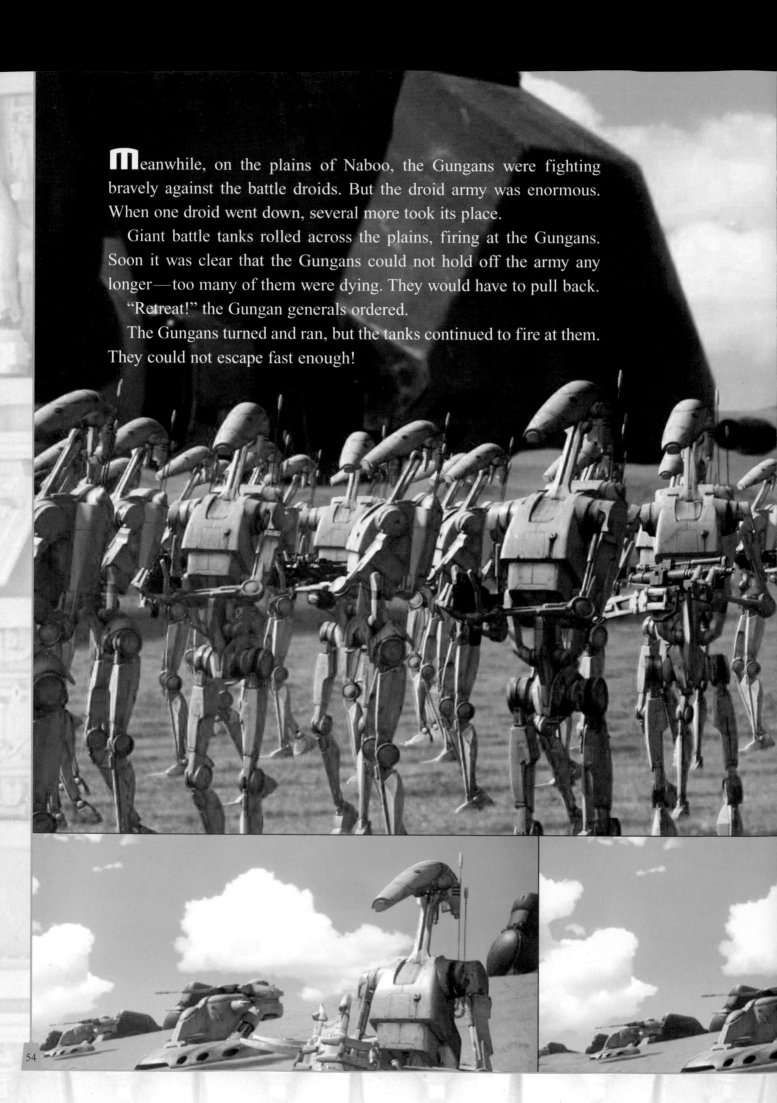

Meanwhile, on the plains of Naboo, the Gungans were fighting bravely against the battle droids. But the droid army was enormous. When one droid went down, several more took its place.

Giant battle tanks rolled across the plains, firing at the Gungans. Soon it was clear that the Gungans could not hold off the army any longer—too many of them were dying. They would have to pull back.

"Retreat!" the Gungan generals ordered.

The Gungans turned and ran, but the tanks continued to fire at them. They could not escape fast enough!

In space, Anakin's ship was on autopilot... and heading right for a huge battleship in the distance.

All around them, ships were firing at one another. Anakin and R2-D2 were flying straight into a starfighter battle!

With a flash of light, a ship exploded to Anakin's right.

"Get us off autopilot, Artoo!" Anakin shouted.

The little droid beeped a reply, and now Anakin was in control! He steered toward a Trade Federation droid starfighter and pressed a button. But instead of firing a weapon, Anakin's ship lurched forward, zooming past the droid ship!

"Whoa!"

Up ahead, the brave Naboo pilots were attacking the giant Trade Federation Control Ship. But the ship was too big, its deflector shield too strong. The pilots didn't stand a chance.

"We'll never get through this shield," one of the pilots reported over his transmitter.

At that moment, Anakin's starfighter was hit. It spun out of control, past the enemy fleet, straight into the Control Ship's hangar.

Anakin was streaking across the deck at top speed!

R2-D2 beeped a warning.

"I'm *trying* to stop!" Anakin shouted back. Then, finally, Anakin's starfighter screeched to a halt. Battle droids swiftly surrounded it.

Anakin and R2-D2 were in *big* trouble.

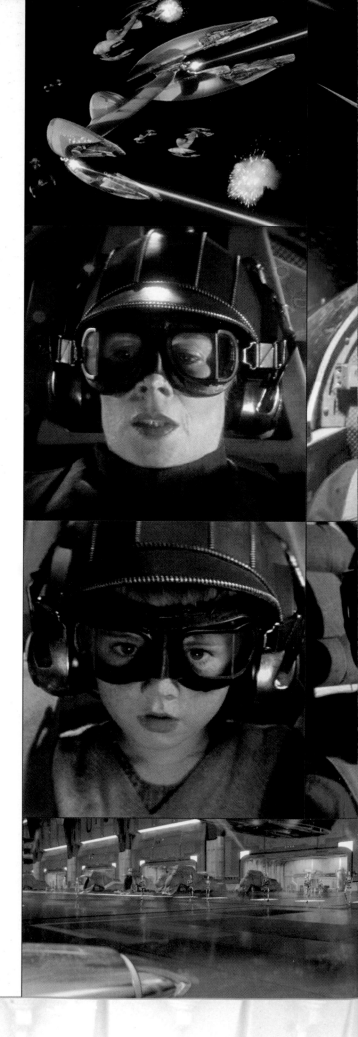

Back on Naboo, Qui-Gon waited patiently in his energy cell. When the beams switched off, he leapt to his feet. Behind him, Obi-Wan tried to catch up to Qui-Gon before the beams re-activated. But the system was too fast. When the beams came on again, Obi-Wan was trapped, just one cell away.

Helplessly, he watched his Master fight the Sith without him.

Qui-Gon's sword flashed as he blocked Darth Maul's fierce blows, but the Jedi was losing strength. Their crackling sabers clashed again and again as they moved toward a large melting pit.

Then, suddenly, Darth Maul caught Qui-Gon off guard. With a lightning-quick move, Maul thrust his lightsaber into Qui-Gon's chest. Qui-Gon dropped heavily to the floor.

"Nooo!" Obi-Wan screamed as the electron gate opened.

Surging forward, Obi-Wan raised his lightsaber as Darth Maul attacked. They battled back and forth.

Soon Obi-Wan grew weary. And a moment later, the Jedi was forced into the melting pit. The Sith Lord smiled evilly as he kicked Obi-Wan's lightsaber down the endless shaft.

Refusing to give up, Obi-Wan summoned all his strength. He leapt out of the pit and called Qui-Gon's lightsaber. It flew into his hands, and Obi-Wan swung with a vengeance, cutting Darth Maul down. The Sith fell screaming into the melting pit, never to emerge again.

Exhausted, Obi-Wan switched off the lightsaber and rushed to his Master's side.

"It's too late for me," Qui-Gon whispered.

"No!" Obi-Wan cried, unwilling to let his Master go.

"Obi-Wan, promise...promise me you'll train the boy."

Obi-Wan struggled to hold back tears as he cradled his Master's head in his lap. "Yes, Master," he promised.

"He is the chosen one..." rasped Qui-Gon. "He will bring balance...train him!"

A moment later, Qui-Gon Jinn died.

In another part of the palace, the Queen and her followers had tried to take back the throne room. But the viceroy's battle droids had taken them prisoner instead.

Now, held at gunpoint inside the throne room, Queen Amidala watched as one of her handmaidens, Sabé, put another part of their battle plan into action.

Dressed as the Queen, Sabé shouted to the viceroy, Nute Gunray, from the doorway, "I will not be signing any treaty. You've lost!"

The viceroy was suddenly confused. *Who was the real Queen?* he wondered.

Sabé rushed away, and Nute panicked. "After her!" he shouted to his mechanical guards. "This one is a decoy!"

While several battle droids rushed after Sabé, Nute faced Amidala. "Your Queen will not get away with this," he sneered.

Amidala sat down on her throne and hit a security button. A panel popped open, and she grabbed two blaster pistols from inside. She tossed one to Captain Panaka, the second to a Naboo officer. Then she took a third pistol and blasted the last of the battle droids.

Queen Amidala cleared her throat. "Now, Viceroy, this is the end of your occupation of Naboo."

Nute Gunray didn't flinch. "Don't be absurd. It won't be long before hundreds of droidekas break in here to rescue me."

In the Trade Federation Control Ship hangar, Anakin and R2-D2 were surrounded by battle droids.

"Come out of there or we'll blast you!" the droid captain ordered.

But Anakin wasn't about to give up now! He flipped a switch and the ship rose into the air, knocking over the droid captain.

"This should stop them!" Anakin fired the lasers as the ship began to turn. "And take this!" He pressed another button, launching two torpedoes. They zoomed past the droids and flew down a hallway.

Boom! The torpedoes hit the Control Ship's reactor room, setting off a series of explosions that rocked the huge Control Ship.

Anakin's eyes went wide. "Let's get out of here!" he shouted. Quickly, Anakin guided his starfighter right over the heads of the battle droids and out of the hangar.

Behind his starfighter, flames of red and orange lit up the black of space as the Trade Federation ship exploded, then disintegrated into dust.

On the Naboo plains, the battle droids suddenly went haywire. They ran in circles, then stopped in their tracks.

Jar Jar gingerly pushed one of the lifeless droids. It toppled over. The droids had lost contact with their masters. Without the Control Ship, the battle was over. Naboo was free!

Before long, a large cruiser landed in Naboo's main hangar. The doors opened, and the newly elected Chancellor Palpatine disembarked, followed by Yoda, Mace Windu, and other Jedi Council members.

"Your boldness has saved our people," Chancellor Palpatine told the Queen. "Together we shall bring peace and prosperity to the Republic."

A huge parade was held to honor the great victory. It was a festive celebration. But though the Republic was safe for the moment, the Jedi Council knew that somewhere out there lurked a dark, dangerous power.

"There is no doubt. The mysterious warrior was a Sith," Mace Windu said.

"Always two, there are," Yoda warned his fellow Jedi, "a master and an apprentice."

They would have to be on the lookout for the one Sith who remained.

Qui-Gon's death was a loss felt by everyone, but his desire to have Anakin trained as a Jedi would be fulfilled after all. The Jedi Council had given Obi-Wan permission to train young Anakin.

"I am your Master now," Obi-Wan told Anakin. "You will become a Jedi. I promise."